Bears Don't Read!

Emma Chichester Clark

Kane Miller
A DIVISION OF EDC PUBLISHING

First American Edition 2015
Kane Miller, A Division of EDC Publishing

Originally published by HarperCollins Publishers Ltd
under the title BEARS DON'T READ!

Text and illustrations copyright
© Emma Chichester Clark 2014

Translation © 2015
Translated under license from
HarperCollins Publishers Ltd

For information contact:
Kane Miller, A Division of EDC Publishing
P.O. Box 470663
Tulsa, OK 74147-0663
www.kanemiller.com
www.edcpub.com
www.usbornebooksandmore.com

Library of Congress Control Number: 2014946662

Printed in China
7 8 9 10
ISBN: 978-1-61067-366-2

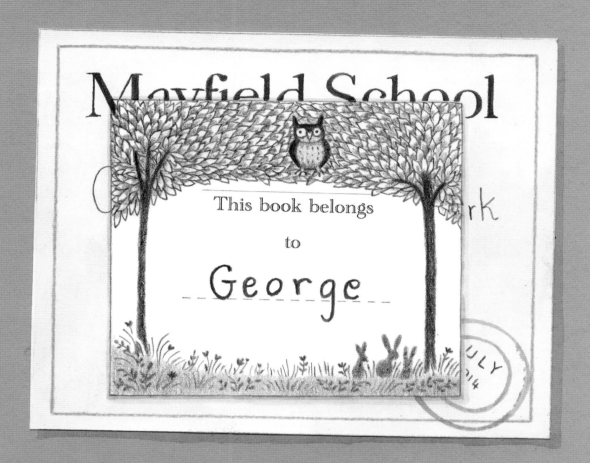

Mayfield School

This book belongs
to
George

Most days, George sat on a bench at the edge
of the woods and stared out at the distant hills.
He wondered about Life.

Oh, life is lovely, he thought. Tra-la-la and all that!
But is this it? he wondered. Is this all there is?

His brothers and sisters never wondered about anything. They were perfectly happy chatting, fishing – doing the usual bear things – and telling the same old stories over and over again.

But George was bored. He didn't want to do the usual bear things anymore. He wanted other things. But *what?* he wondered.

Then, one day, as George was strolling through the forest, he found a book lying beneath a tree.

Somebody must have lost it, he thought. How interesting!
Inside it were pictures of a bear – just like him.

On the other pages there were lots and lots of words.

Each one, even the tiny ones, is saying *something*, he thought. If only I knew what it was... and this bear is having an exciting life, not like mine! George sighed.

But then, he had a brilliant idea!

He rushed home to tell the others.

"I'm going to town to find the owner of this book and ask them to teach me to read!" he said.

"You don't want to go there!" said his brother. "They don't like bears in town."

"But I want to learn to *read!*" said George.

"That's just silly!" said his sister. "Bears don't read! Why can't you be happy doing normal bear things?"

But George would not be put off. He waved good-bye and headed towards the long road into town with the book under his arm.

George walked for a whole day and a whole night,
stopping to rest on a grassy hill under the sparkling sky.

Before he slept he opened the book again and gazed
at the words. Already he felt that the world was a
more interesting place.

The next morning, George rose with the sun and by
midday he could see the town in the distance.
He smiled. It looked lovely.

There must be so many people who know
how to read there, he thought, and lots of
new stories they can tell me.

But when he arrived everyone was running! Some were even screaming! "WAIT!" cried George.

He showed the book to a woman rushing by. "Do you know whose this is?" he asked. "It's from the schoool!" she shrieked and pointed to the red building.

"BEAR!" somebody shouted. "Call the police!"
How peculiar! thought George as he walked
towards the school.

Inside the school, there was complete silence. Where was everybody?

George peered over the desk.

"Hello!" he said, but there was nobody there.

Suddenly, there was a shout.
"Freeze! Hands above your head!"
George was surrounded by policemen!
"What's the matter?" he asked nervously.

"You're a gigantic, great grizzly bear!"
shouted the Chief of Police. "That's the matter!"
They moved towards him, holding up their shields.

"I don't want any trouble!"
said the Chief.

George didn't want any trouble either.

It wasn't his fault he was a
gigantic, great grizzly bear!

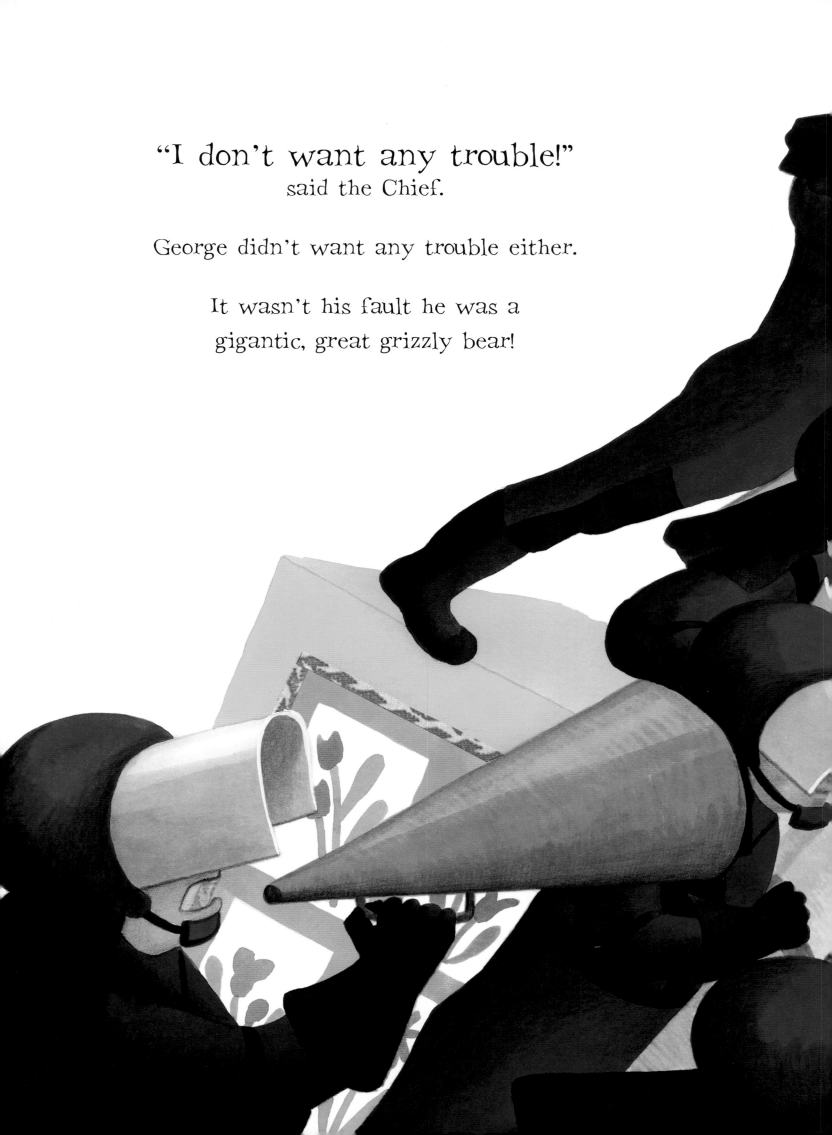

He held the book tightly in his paw.

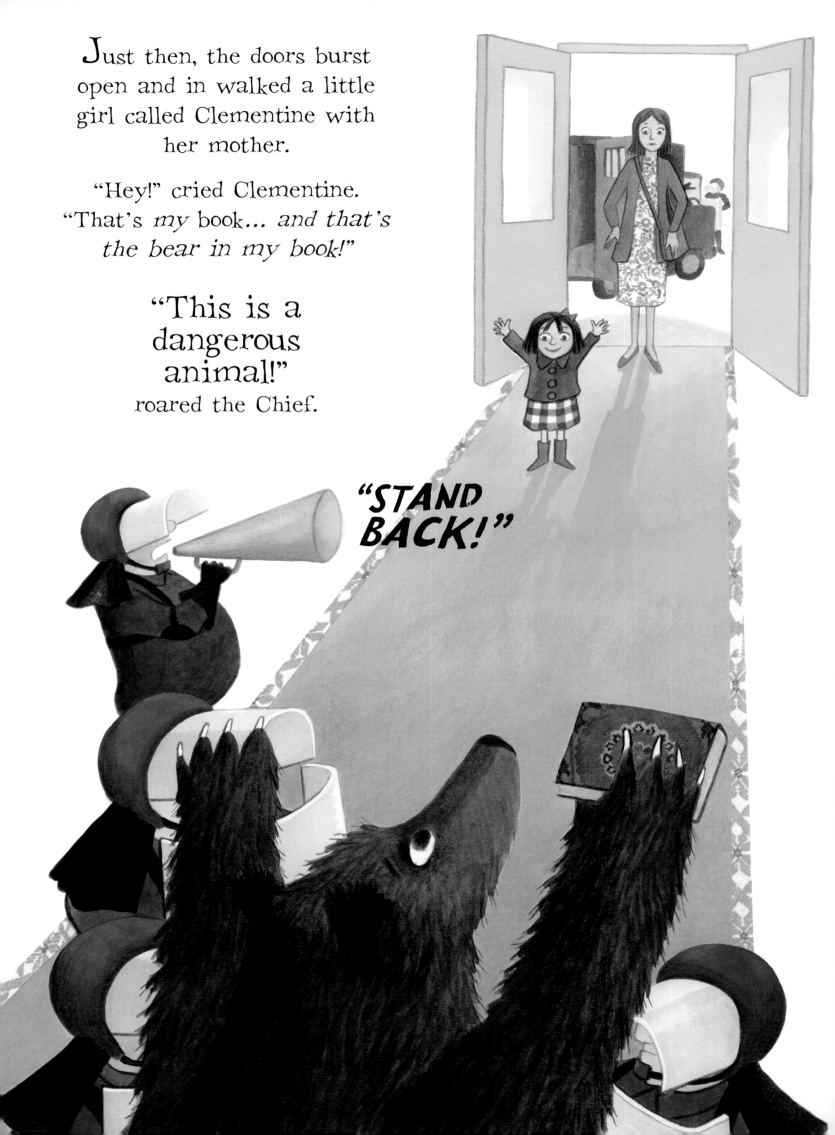

Just then, the doors burst open and in walked a little girl called Clementine with her mother.

"Hey!" cried Clementine. "That's *my* book... *and that's the bear in my book!*"

"This is a dangerous animal!" roared the Chief.

"STAND BACK!"

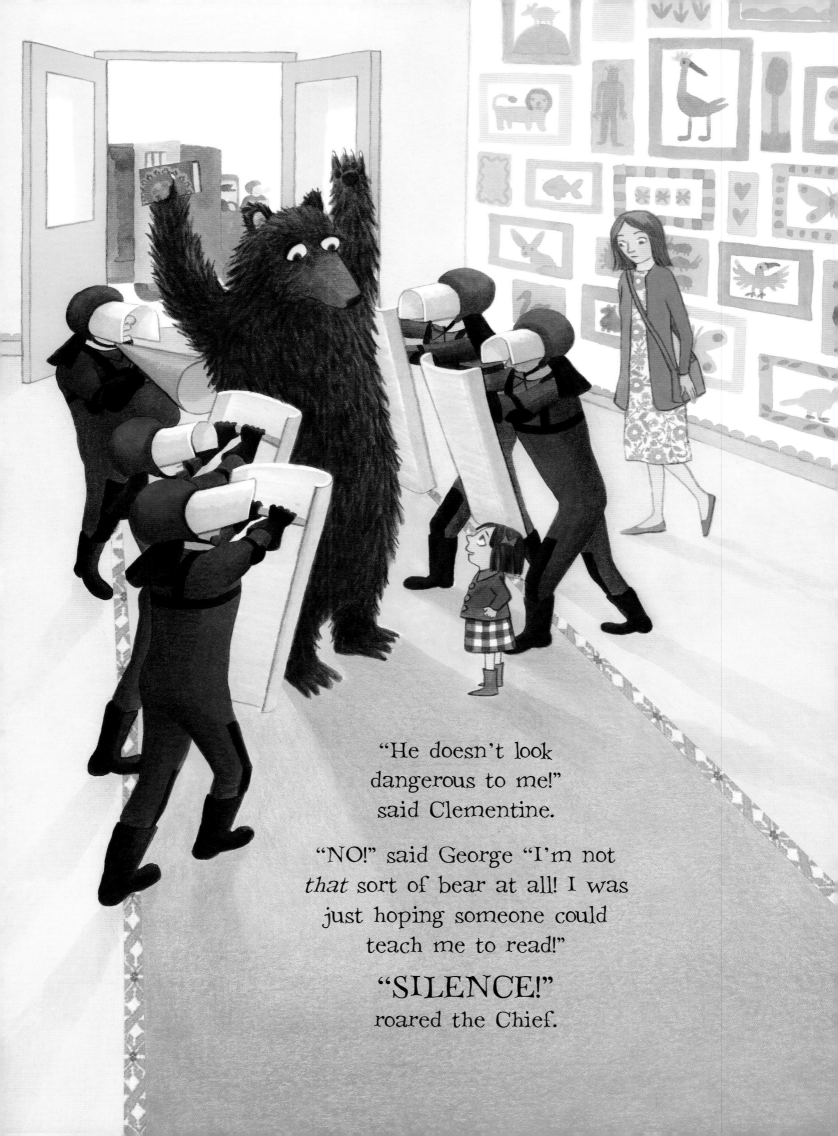

"He doesn't look
dangerous to me!"
said Clementine.

"NO!" said George "I'm not
that sort of bear at all! I was
just hoping someone could
teach me to read!"

"SILENCE!"
roared the Chief.

But Clementine wasn't listening.

"I'm learning to read," she said.
"We could learn together, couldn't we, Mom?"

Clementine's mother looked at George.
She could see he was a perfectly nice
sort of bear.

"I don't see why not!" she said.

"So you'll take responsibility for this bear, will you, madam?" asked the Chief.

"Certainly!" said Clementine's mother. "And there's no need to shout!"

She held out her hand to George.

"Very pleased to meet you," she said.
"Delighted to meet you too!" said George.

George moved into the
summerhouse at the end of
Clementine's garden and each day,
after school, Clementine showed
him everything she'd learned.

It wasn't long before George knew
all the letters of the alphabet.

George didn't find reading easy at first. Even though he tried hard he often made mistakes but, luckily, Clementine was a kind and patient teacher.

Sometimes the Chief came to see how they were getting on. He brought a book of his favorite poetry to read aloud to George.

"My love is like a red, red rose..."

Then one day, Clementine said,
"I bet you can read this whole book now,
all by yourself!"

George opened it and began,

*"Once upon a time,
there was a large
brown bear who
found a book lying
under a tree..."*

He read the whole book, all the way to the end.
"Bravo!" said Clementine. "We knew you could do it!"

And for George – that was just the beginning.